Tilly

and the TROUBLE in the Night

HILARY McKAY

ILLUSTRATED BY KIMBERLEY SCOTT

For Phoebe and Gabriel,
With love from Hilary
H.M.

To my monkey, James
K.S.

EGMONT
We bring stories to life

Book Band: Gold
This edition first published in Great Britain 2013
by Egmont UK Ltd
The Yellow Building, 1 Nicholas Road, London W11 4AN.
Text copyright © Hilary McKay 2013
Illustrations copyright © Kimberley Scott 2013
The author and illustrator have asserted their moral rights.
ISBN 978 1 4052 6720 5
10 9 8 7 6 5 4 3 2 1
A CIP catalogue record for this title is available from the British Library.
Printed in Singapore.
55193/1

EGMONT LUCKY COIN

Our story began over a century ago, when seventeen-year-old
Egmont Harald Petersen found a coin in the street.

He was on his way to buy a flyswatter, a small hand-operated
printing machine that he then set up in his tiny apartment.

The coin brought him such good luck that today Egmont has
offices in over 30 countries around the world. And that lucky
coin is still kept at the company's head offices in Denmark.

CONTENTS

One, Two, Three, Four, Five!   5

Something Else   13

EBay and the Rock Band   21

To eBay, or not to eBay?   29

The Boss Around Here   39

Red Bananas

1 Tilly & Family

2 Granny

3 The Doctor

4 Uncle Kevin

5 The Rough Lot

M

N Great Uncle Max

Timmy

ONE, TWO, THREE, FOUR, FIVE!

There were four people at Tilly's house:

Tilly's father, who was a maths teacher.

Tilly's mother, who tried to write books.

Tilly's little brother Timmy, who sucked his thumb when he was tired.

And Tilly, who had red hair and lots of good ideas.

Tilly had taught Timmy to count.

'One, two, three, four,' said Timmy, counting the people in the house.

'Good!' said Tilly.

'Five!' said Timmy, and he looked at the door as if someone had just come in. But there wasn't anyone that Tilly could see.

Soon after this things began to change at Tilly's house. Timmy, who so far had been nearly always good, now became the opposite. Nearly always bad.

Not in the daytime. In the daytime he took grumpy naps.

But at night he was terribly noisy.

He sang.

He jumped on his bed.

He raced cars on the landing and sailed boats in the bath and built farms on the stairs and he ran about shouting.

Nobody knew why.

And nobody could sleep.

It was very hard for Timmy's father to teach maths. He got so sleepy he couldn't see the numbers.

It was very hard for Timmy's mother to write books. She got so sleepy she couldn't see the letters.

At school Tilly yawned so much she couldn't
see the numbers or the letters or anything else.

Tilly's family took Timmy to the doctors.
The doctor looked at the front of Timmy
and the back of Timmy and in Timmy's ears.
He took Timmy's thumb out of his mouth and
looked down his throat. He listened while
Timmy counted to five. Then he said,
'Timmy is a very healthy boy indeed.'

'Can't he have some medicine to make him go to sleep?' asked Timmy's father.

'No he can't,' said the doctor.

'Then can we have some medicine to make us stay awake?' asked Timmy's mother.

'Certainly not!' said the doctor.

'Do you think it is an illness making Timmy stay awake all night?' asked Tilly, looking hard at the doctor.

'No,' said the doctor, looking hard at Tilly. 'I don't. I think it is something else.'

Something else, thought Tilly, and she looked at Timmy and she wondered.

Hmm . . .

SOMETHING ELSE

Bedtime came while Tilly was still wondering.

'Bedtime!' she said to Timmy.

'I don't want to,' said Timmy.

'Yes you do,' said Tilly. 'Nice splashy bath!
Nice get-lost-in-them towels! Nice raggy
pyjamas! Nice bedtime story! And then off you
pop to sleep!'

'No I don't,' said Timmy.

'No you don't,' agreed Tilly. 'Not any more.
Why not?'

'My friend doesn't like bedtime,' said Timmy.

'What friend?' asked Tilly.

Timmy thought for a while, and then he said, 'Morgan.'

'Morgan?' asked Tilly.

'Naughty Morgan,' said Timmy.

'I didn't know you had a friend called Naughty Morgan,' said Tilly.

'That's because you can't see him,' said Timmy.

Then Tilly noticed that Timmy was lying very oddly in his bed. All on one side. There was a space beside Timmy where another person could fit. There was a place on Timmy's pillow where another head could lie.

'Does Naughty Morgan sleep in your bed at night?' asked Tilly.

'No,' said Timmy. 'Naughty Morgan doesn't sleep anywhere at night. He likes to stay up all night. He is just lying there right now, waiting.'

'Waiting for what?' asked Tilly.

'Waiting for you to go,' said Timmy.

'Then what will he do?' asked Tilly.

Timmy turned to the empty space beside his pillow. He asked, 'What will you do when Tilly has gone?' He listened for a reply. Then he said to Tilly, 'Hammer!'

'Hammer?' asked Tilly.

'Yes, and I will help him,' said Timmy. 'If that's all right.'

'No it isn't all right!' said Tilly.

'I was talking to Naughty Morgan, not you,' said Timmy. 'Naughty Morgan is the boss around here.'

'I shall be very cross if Naughty Morgan keeps everyone awake all night,' said Tilly.

'Naughty Morgan won't care,' said Timmy. 'He likes people being cross. Naughty Morgan isn't scared of anything except one thing and he won't tell me what it is. What story are you going to read us tonight?'

'*The Three Bears,*' said Tilly.

You will like this one . . .

The Three Bears

Timmy turned to the space on his pillow where Naughty Morgan's head might be and asked, 'Is that OK?' Then he listened, then he nodded.

'*The Three Bears* is OK,' he told Tilly.

So Tilly read the story of the Three Bears and then she kissed Timmy goodnight (Naughty Morgan would not be kissed) and she went downstairs and told her parents all she had found out.

'Timmy has an invisible new friend,' she explained. 'His name is Naughty Morgan and he likes to stay up all night. It's no good being cross because he likes people being cross. He isn't scared of anything except one thing and he is the boss around here.'

Tilly's father and mother were very upset to hear this bad news. They were very fond of Timmy.

'But what can we do?' they asked. 'We can't teach sums with no sleep. We can't write books with no sleep. And Tilly can't go to school and learn things with no sleep. We will have to sell poor little Timmy on eBay. It seems so sad. He was such a good little boy.'

Everyone went to bed very unhappily that night. They went to bed, but they did not sleep, because of the hammering.

EBAY AND THE ROCK BAND

Tilly spent the night thinking hard.

Early in the morning she said, 'Don't let's sell Timmy on eBay just yet. Let's send him on a visit to dear old Granny. Perhaps he will be good there, away from Naughty Morgan.'

'Perhaps,' said Tilly's parents doubtfully.

'It's worth a try,' said Tilly, and she rushed to pack up Timmy's things at once.

'You will have a lovely time,' she told Timmy.

'But . . .' said Timmy.

'Just you and dear old Granny!'

'But . . .' said Timmy.

'And I will come every night to read your bedtime story.'

'Oh, all right,' said Timmy with his thumb in his mouth.

Granny was very pleased to see Timmy. She said that he could stay as long as he liked.

Thank goodness! thought Tilly, as she hurried off to school. All day she thought about Timmy and Granny, and in the evening she went back to see how they were.

'Timmy has been perfectly good!' said dear old Granny. 'First he had a nice long nap. Then he had his lunch. Then he had another nice long nap. Then he had his tea.

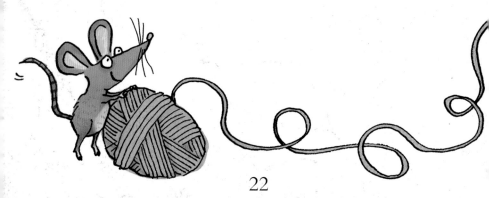

Yummy!

He couldn't have been less trouble. It would be a dreadful waste to sell such a good little boy on eBay!'

'Where is he now?' asked Tilly.

'Upstairs, in bed, waiting for his story,' Granny told her.

So Tilly went upstairs and there was Timmy looking very comfy in Granny's spare bed. Tilly was pleased to see that he was right in the middle, with no space for anyone beside him.

'What story is it tonight?' asked Timmy.

'*The Three Little Pigs and the Big Bad Wolf,*' said Tilly.

'Oh,' said Timmy, and he turned upside down in bed, hung over the edge, and spoke into the space underneath.

Listened for a reply.

Sat up again.

'Pigs are all right,' he told Tilly. 'Wolves too!'

'Timmy,' said Tilly, 'did Naughty Morgan come with you to Granny's house?'

'Course he did!' said Timmy. 'He's my friend! Hurry up with our story!'

So Tilly hurried up with the story and then she hugged Timmy (but not Naughty Morgan, who didn't like hugs) and she said, 'Goodnight. I hope you sleep well.'

'I hope we don't,' said Timmy cheerfully.

'Naughty Morgan says this would be a very good place for a rock band.'

'Not a rock band!' said Tilly, horrified. 'Dear old Granny would go wild!'

'Naughty Morgan loves wild people!' said Timmy. 'The wilder the better, Naughty Morgan says! He's not afraid of anything except one thing that I don't know, and he's the boss around here!'

Tilly went home rather thoughtfully.

And she was right to be thoughtful.

One night of listening to Naughty Morgan's rock band changed Granny's mind completely.

'Take Timmy away and put him on eBay at once!' she ordered. 'I've never had such a terrible night.'

'Oh, Timmy!' said Tilly.

'Naughty Morgan made me,' said Timmy.

'Naughty Morgan made him,' said Tilly pleadingly to Granny.

'Then put Naughty Morgan on eBay too!' said Granny.

TO EBAY, OR NOT TO EBAY?

That was the question. Granny said eBay.
Tilly's father and mother said eBay. But
Tilly didn't agree. Instead she took Timmy
to Uncle Kevin's house. Uncle Kevin's house
was very like a castle,
with swans in the moat
and peacocks on the
drawbridge and
flags on the
turrets.

'Golly gosh!'
said Uncle Kevin.

'Of course young Tim can live with me! Spot on! Perfect! You can't sell a little chap like that on eBay!'

'He's sometimes a tiny bit noisy at night,' said Tilly.

'Snore m'self!' said Uncle Kevin. 'Him and me will get on fine! Won't we, Tim old man?'

'Yeth,' said Timmy with his thumb in his mouth.

'Wonderful!' said Tilly, and ran off to school.

I bet he's good all day, she thought.

She was right. Timmy spent the day snoozing in the shade of the castle walls and only waking up for jam sandwiches.

When Tilly came back at bedtime she found
him sitting in a hammock hung up in the
library and waiting for his story.

'What is it?' he asked.

'*Snow White and the Seven Spiders*,' said Tilly.

'Dwarves!' said Timmy.

'No, I think spiders,' said Tilly.

'Spiders OK?' Timmy asked the armchair by the fire, listened, and then nodded.

So Tilly read the story of *Snow White and the Seven Spiders* and afterwards she said goodnight to Timmy.

'Sleep well!' she said, swinging him in his hammock.

'I probably won't have time,' said Timmy. 'Naughty Morgan says this is the best place in the world for mountaineering practice!'

'No, Timmy!' said Tilly, gazing in horror at the shelves and shelves of enormous books, stretching high into the dimness of the library ceiling. 'Uncle Kevin would go bonkers!'

'Uncle Kevin is bonkers!' said Timmy. 'And he doesn't frighten Naughty Morgan. Naughty Morgan isn't scared of anything except one thing! Are you going now?'

'I suppose so,' said Tilly. 'Timmy?'

'Yes?'

'Do you have to do what Naughty Morgan says?'

'Yes,' said Timmy, smiling sweetly. 'I do. Naughty Morgan is the boss around here.'

Tilly went home expecting the worst. And she was right to do that. In the morning, there was Uncle Kevin dancing with rage among the ruins of his library.

There were ten thousand books, tumbled on the floor.

There was Timmy, with his thumb in his mouth.

'First I thought it was thunder!' complained Uncle Kevin. 'Then I thought thunder AND the roof falling off. Then I thought thunder AND the roof falling off AND an earthquake! Take him away and put him on eBay RIGHT NOW!'

But still Tilly could not bear to do that
sensible thing. Instead she took Timmy across
town to where their cousins, the Rough Lot,
lived. Their house was so noisy and messy
and stuffed full of people that she hoped they
wouldn't mind one more.

And they didn't.

(At first.)

The Rough Lot found Timmy a sleeping
bag and a nice patch of floor and they all ate
chips and curry sauce while Tilly read the
interesting story of *Beauty and the Beast*.

And then Tilly went away, and in the morning she came back.

And there was Timmy, sitting on the doorstep with a notice hanging over his head:

Free to Good Home

'We thought it would be quicker than eBay,' the Rough Lot said.

'But why?' asked Tilly.

'Only because,' said Timmy with his thumb in his mouth, 'Naughty Morgan and me tried to teach the dogs to sing. It was Naughty Morgan's idea. He thought of it and he made me!'

'The police came!' the Rough Lot told Tilly. 'The neighbours called them! But they couldn't do anything to make it stop.'

'Course they couldn't,' said Timmy. 'Naughty Morgan's the boss around here!'

THE BOSS AROUND HERE

So Tilly took Timmy to their very last relation. Great Uncle Max.

And Great Uncle Max was out.

'Bother!' said Tilly.

'Not bother,' said Timmy, standing on tiptoe to peer over the garden gate. 'Good.'

Great Uncle
Max

IS
OUT

'Good?' asked Tilly.

'Yes, cos Naughty Morgan says this is just the place for an all-night party!'

'No,' said Tilly. 'Tonight there will be no all-night party! No teaching dogs to sing! No mountaineering! No rock bands! No hammering!'

'What will there be, then?' asked Timmy.

'Tonight there will be a nice splashy bath,' said Tilly. 'Nice get-lost-in-them towels. Nice raggy pyjamas. And a nice bedtime story.'

'What will the story be?' asked Timmy.

'*George and the Dragon*,' said Tilly.

'Oh,' said Timmy, and he looked over his shoulder at a place where Tilly could not see anyone standing and listened for a while.

Then he shook his head.

'Naughty Morgan says not *that* story,' he told Tilly. 'And he says you'd better think of another one because he's the boss around here.'

'Mmmm,' said Tilly thoughtfully and then she said, 'Aaah!' and she took Timmy home to their father and mother (who were quite alarmed to see him).

'Don't worry,' said Tilly. 'Everything will be all right. I'm just popping out for a few minutes now.'

'Why?' asked Tilly's parents, kissing Timmy nervously.

One, two, three ... Heave!

'There is something I need to collect,' said Tilly.

Whatever Tilly collected she took up to her bedroom, where it only just fitted.

And then it was bedtime, so she read Timmy
a nice quiet story about tigers.

'Tigers?' Timmy asked the space beside his
head. Listened. Nodded.

'Naughty Morgan likes tigers,' he said.

'Good,' said Tilly, and after the story she
tucked Timmy up very gently, and she tucked
Naughty Morgan up too, even though he
didn't like it.

'Now,' said Tilly. 'Go to sleep as fast as you can and for goodness' sake be good. There's something in my bedroom you mustn't wake up.'

'What?' asked Timmy.

'I don't want to tell you in case I scare Naughty Morgan,' said Tilly.

'Naughty Morgan,' began Timmy, 'is not scared of anything . . .'

'Except one thing,' said Tilly.

When Timmy's bedroom door was open he could see across the landing to Tilly's own door. Tilly opened Timmy's door wide, and she opened hers just a crack.

Which was all it would open, because of what was inside.

But just a crack was enough . . .

'A DRAGON!' Timmy told Naughty Morgan in a horrified whisper.

'Yes,' said Tilly, gently closing her door again. 'So you'd better be quiet. Because that dragon is the boss around here!'

In the morning, after that long peaceful night, Timmy practised his counting again.

'One, two, three, four.'

Tilly waited for him to say five, but he didn't. He stopped. And then he looked at the door as if someone had just gone out.

And that was the end of the trouble in the night at Tilly's house.